KINGS ARE BORN

ONUOHA K. EMEABA

SKEENFON Communications Limited

CHAPTER ONE

The sky was gloomy, with clouds hovering over the air. There was a grave silence as the night grew cold and colder beneath and darkness covered the face of the earth. Only sounds of hollow drums and harsh trumpets from spirits making a guffaw to the graveyard could be heard. It was like the ancestors were meeting in the village square as the entire kingdom went into absolute calmness. Ancestors seldom meet, but when they meet, no human being would be seen outside eavesdropping on their deliberations. People would withdrew to their various houses. Only those with dual citizenship of the spirit and mortal could go out to perform their daily communication.

It was axiomatic that ancestors meetings bestow good climate as the moon usually peeped through the sky to watch the mother earth hosting the ancestors. It was also believed that *Usumani* River usually overflowed its banks to greet the ancestors. And those ancient diviners derive inspiration from the meeting of the ancestors.

The dreadful weather was observed with mixed grill as the grave stillness persisted for a while and the priest of *Kalu-nde-ebe* had started consulting the oracle to conjure the gods.

"Kookorokoo" the rooster crowed to pronounce the crack of dawn. But the weather looked like the night was only half spent.

After the second cock crow, the atmosphere changed from calmness to that of chaos. The village began to crack in aggressive and stubborn wind with successive sound of roaring thunder tearing the sky. It came hurrying with heavy wind and rainfall. Great water drops were dribbling and droning with insistent devotion upon roofs. There were lightning and thunderstorm. And people were cornered by the fear gnawing at their heart. The rain bellowed and beat her chest angrily as the accomplished wind rummaged about the villages and provoked the big *"Achi"* tree at the village square to produce aggressive and stubborn flying tree branches.

Achi Tree

It was an *Nkwor* day, when everybody in the village was expected to be in the market with their wares. Only children were usually seen in compounds on *Nkwor* days. They would be doing the house chores like scrubbing the floors and painting the walls with new leafs after fetching water from the stream. People were forbidden from going to the farm on *Nkwo* days. Everyone looked forward to see the *Nkwor* day as it went with merry-making.

But this *Nkwor* day was different, it was full of sorrow. The severe weather came with early rainstorm that destroyed properties in the village and distressed the people. While the people were still howling over the calamitous confrontation, the town crier went round the village to announce the meeting of kingmakers. He announced that any member of the palace that was found absent in meeting would be adequately penalized.

Town Crier

The town crier as the medium between the village and the palace had respect bestowed on him thus making his announcements definite. There was an air of reverence for the town crier as he went round the village to do his duty.

It was already mid-morning, as members of the king makers were anxiously gathering. They were grieved by an inkling of the matter for deliberation in the meeting. Some of them construed the weather condition as a bad omen as calamity and doom were written all over their faces.

CHAPTER TWO

Members of the palace were seated in their ranks. The palace was a mighty edifice that was built many years ago by communal effort. It was built to accommodate representatives of the constituent villages that made up the kingdom. The *Ituezes* and *Isieyes* were the legislative arms of the palace. The *Ituezes* were responsible for policy making while the *Isieyes* ratify the policies and the clan rulers implement the policies in their various clans. The *Ituezes* were seated in the right flank and the *Isieyes* in the left. At the pavilion were the rulers of the five clans. The Chief Priest was at the end of the parlour with two of his tyros standing behind him. The two men were carrying raffia bags and roosters.

Okonta-nwa-Otamba, tall and huge as a hill, was standing at the center of the parlour. He had a broad nose and thick lips with eyeballs that gave him a distinctive African posture. Okonta was known as a great warrior who used to tear men like garment in battles. From a young age, Okonta had fought many battles for the people of Ukpaghari. And he was never defeated in any of the battles. His contemporaries used to call him *seven-men-in-one-man*. This nickname was evidenced in his broad chest and well-toned upper arm muscles. Okonta was a stutterer who believed in action than rhetoric.

He was beating his chest and gesturing as he was struggling to convince members of the palace to consider his request. He seldom laughed except when there was an imminent war. His face was beaming a bogus laughter to the apprehension of the palace members. Still beating his chest, he continued his speech.

"I, Ichie Okonta-nwa-Otamba, the Achi of Ukpaghari, the lion of our kingdom is here to make my will known to you," Okonta thundered and his elephant sized body seemed to force the words on the people. He regarded them and murmured some words. In utter bewilderment, the crowd applauded his utterances and urged him on.

Speaker of the Clans signaled the crowd to be quiet. He stood and greeted "Chacha Ukpaghari kwenu!" He repeated the greeting three times and the crowd corresponded with their responses. He turned to Okonta and urged him to continue with his speech and avoid vain words.

"Thank you my lords. I must say my will… If it is good, please lend me your support, but if you found it not good enough…you should consider my status in the kingdom—an Iroko tree can never be disregarded in the forest."

He was gasping out the words when the speaker of the clans reprimanded him for incoherent statements. Okonta looked askance on the speaker and regarded him with a daring smile.

He gave a moment silence as the meeting went into a din and abruptly started fuming in anger before Iwuoha interrupted him again.

"Cha! Cha! Cha! Ukpaghari kwenu!" Iwuoha saluted three times and the crowd gave corresponding reply "Hooa" after every salute. He gave a moment silence and began to address the palace:

"Our elders said that he who holds his debtor on the ground holds himself.

Let us not make our son Okonta swallow his words in a bid to force it out of his mouth." He turned to Okonta and advised him to go right into the crux of his message.

Iwuoha was a middle-aged witty man that commanded great respect for his rhetorical carriage. He never lacked words to calm turbulent situations. And he seldom wasted his breath without achieving his aim. He abruptly brought the uproar to normalcy and urged Okonta to continue.

"I greet you my lords", Okonta continued, If we did not raise a noise like this, it would look like the dead were meeting in this place."

He was still talking when Okafor, the Chief Priest interrupted him. "The gods are hungry for your words," the Chief priest mumbled.

Chief Priest

The Chief Priest was always in the mood of divination. His words were those of the gods. He was the medium through which the dead and the living communicated. His physical outlook described his dual citizenship of the dead and the living. The right part of his body was decorated with white chalk while the left was black. The white part was for the physical world while the black was for the unseen world. And he belonged to the two worlds.

Everybody in Ukpaghari kingdom dreaded

Okafor like a plague except Okonta. He believed that Okafor's divinations were a lazy man's art. To Okonta, only men of great gallantry deserved recognition in any gathering.

Okonta regarded Okafor with disdain and continued his speech. He raised his palm and beat his chest and thundered like a roaring lion, "I, the strength of Ukpaghari kingdom, the icon of Ogirigbuo, the god of thunder wants to be the king of the land. This is my word." He heaved a sigh of relief as the palace went into another round of momentary silence.

"Cha! Cha! Cha! Umu Ukpaghari kwenu!" Okonta greeted and the crowd was frozen to silence. He saluted the crowd three times without the complimentary response. It was an unprecedented action that left the people bemused.

While the people were still bereft of action, Okechie, the speaker of the *Ituezes* stood vehemently to suggest that Okonta-nwa-Otamba be thrown out of the palace for insulting the nobility of the palace.

"This man should be discarded into the evil forest because he is possessed of the evil spirit" Okechie retorted in a furious anger.

"Incredible," Okonta snapped at the speaker. "So this little bird has weighed itself and felt it could fight its god." He was talking irreverently and moving towards the speaker as if to pounce on him. The palace went into a bedlam. Okonta's movement meant calamity. If Okonta would pounce on any of the wrinkle-ridden old men, he would crush the person's bones. And he was actually moving to grab the speaker when Okafor, the Chief priest interfered with his shrilling utterance.

"Okonta the brave one; the gods are angry with you. You should…" he could not finish his message before Okonta spontaneously responded,

"Tell your gods to go to the ancestors with their messages"

The palace could not wait to perform the closing protocols of palace meetings before the members started leaping out of the palace in a riotous mood. But before the Chief priest could step out of the palace, he sounded a warning that Okonta pinched the gods and that they await him in the festival of the seventh moon. In a corresponding manner, members of the palace were hurriedly moving out with bitter remarks of Okonta's desecration of the palace.

In an obvious feeling of defeat, Okonta made to grab and tear any of the old men to satisfy his ego as they were moving out of the palace. Iwuoha had a feeling of his thinking and quickly moved to him and began to psyche him with soothing words.

"Okonta-nwa-Otamba! You are the brave man of Ukpaghari. Neighboring communities tremble at the mention of your name in a battle. It is only a foolish man that could dare the power of the brave Okonta in any battle."

Iwuoha also warned Okonta that a brave man who kills his father, kills his power and that the noble members of the palace were the fathers and pride of Okonta's power.

Okonta was left in a fit of anger as everybody deserted the palace. He waited for a while pondering on what to do in order to achieve his goal. Okonta was believed to have more life in his muscle than in his brain and that he usually acts before thinking. He stood with his head jerked upright and arms folded across his chest.

CHAPTER THREE

The evening was calm. Life had crept back to the village. Domestic animals were returning from scavenging for food and going into their nests. Children were helping their parents in doing domestic chores. The female ones were in the kitchen helping their mothers in preparing dinners while the boys were in the huts with their fathers. After their dinner, children would go out for the moonlight play in the village square.

Okonta's compound was lively with activities. Domestic animals were rummaging round the large compound, howling, hissing and crowing. Rays of light that were beaming from the three kitchens enlivened the entire compound.

The large compound had a gigantic hut that served as main entrance as well as Okonta's sitting room. The hut also comprised his bedroom and extra rooms for visitors. Nobody would get into the compound without passing through the hut. Each of Okonta's wives, Mgborie, Ogbenyealu and Chika had their kitchens that contained a room with a mud bed. They cook foods in the inner room that was the actual kitchen and entertain visitors in the outer room. In the night, the women sleep in the mud beds with their children. But the male children always slept with their father in the main parlor.

Mgborie, Ogbenyealu and Chika were in the main parlor. They were anticipating their husband's success in the palace meeting. "Hmmm, hell will befall the kingdom if the palace fails to favour our husband today" Ogbenyealu remarked. She strongly believed that Okonta as a warrior was the best contender for the throne of *Ukpa*. Ogbenyealu grew up in Ukpaghari kingdom and knew everything about Okonta. She knew how he dealt with neighboring communities and how he single-handedly repelled enemies' efforts to annex a portion of the Ukpaghari Kingdom. The singular effort endeared him to everybody in the Kingdom. Also, Okonta was a famous wrestler in his youth age. No youth from any of the neighboring communities that dared him, went undefeated. While Ogbenyealu was recounting these features of Okonta to his other wives, she noted that it was his bravado that lured her into marrying him.

Ogbenyealu was the belle of her time. She was tall, huge and well-built with hips that gave her a perfect beauty. Ogbenyealu was not only stunning; she was equally believed to be courteous. Wealthy people in the land tried to woo her into marriage, but Okonta won her heart with his gallantry in surprisingly defeating neighboring communities, and protecting Ukpaghari kingdom. It had been more than fifteen years since Ogbenyealu married Okonta. Her love and respect for Okonta had grown stronger in these years. She believed that Okonta had the charisma of being the sovereign head of the Kingdom.

Mgborie equally believed in Okonta. She believed that Okonta had all that was required to rule the famous land of Ukpaghari. She had ample knowledge of Okonta since she was the first wife. Mgborie was not from Ukpaghari, but she had lived in the kingdom for more than twenty years when she was given to Okonta for marriage. She was the princess of Okeofia and was given to Okonta for reparation by Okeofia people when a daughter of Ukpaghari was assassinated in Okeofia community. The woman went to sell her farm products in Okeofia when she was assassinated in the place. Okonta was to lead a reprisal attack on Okeofia community. When an emissary was dispatched to the king of Okeofia, he opted to pay with her daughter than incurring wrath of Okonta.

Okonta was very youthful when Mgborie was brought to him for compensation. He was to lead the team that would sacrifice the damsel to appease the land of Ukpaghari for the blood of an innocent Ukpaghari woman that was spilled by Okeofia people. They decided to keep the damsel in Okonta's custody to guard against the warriors of Okeofia invading the kingdom to rescue the princess. She had stayed in Okonta's house for six days. On the seventh day when the priest of *kamalu agbaramini* was to lead the killing of the

Mgborie, Okonta opted to marry her and compensate the family of the deceased woman.

Sequel to this request, Okonta was asked to pay dowry to the family of the woman that was assassinated in Okeofia. He also paid all that the chief priest requested to appease the land before he married Mgborie.

In return, Mgborie owed her life to Okonta. She loved Okonta so much and revered him to the extent that she was calling him *"My lord."* And her marriage with Okonta was blessed with two children, a boy and a girl.

Her great fear and respect for Okonta influenced her contributions in any discussion on the warrior. Mgborie craved that Okonta would be favoured in the palace meeting. She also expressed great fear on what Okonta's reaction would be if the people decided not to favour him. *"In fact heaven will fall if the people fail to crown Okonta-nwa-Otamba as the next Ukpa of Ukpaghari"* Mgborie avowed.

"Nnekudi" Chika was referring to Mgborie the first wife, "your reasoning about our husband is always not realistic. How do you think that our husband could be the king without other people's approval?"

Before she could finish her statement, Mgborie snapped at her "Shut up your mouth! You are still a child," She urged her to adore Okonta-nwa-Otamba for his strength that was above that of everybody else's in the community. Mgborie warned Chika that any person that failed to fear Okonta in the land is challenging his or her "*chi*" in a wrestle. "I don't know what you are talking about because I know that you are suffering from primordial sense of living."

Mgborie misunderstood Chika and thought that she had accused her of suffering from a biological disease. She moved swiftly to strangle Chika when Ogbenyealu intervened and cautioned the two wives against fighting.

"Don't mind this old hen that is still running crazy after the blood of a young rooster." Mgborie became more infuriated with the disdain.

"Ogbenyealu, did you hear this bastard that our husband picked from the bush path, she has the gut to insult me, the first of Okonta's wives" She remarked bitterly. Mgborie had kept this thought in her mind for the past seven years that Okonta brought Chika and unceremoniously announced her as his third wife.

Chika was about a few years older than Uredi, Mgborie's daughter. Okonta picked her from the bush that was leading to Aroukwu, the city where people were sold like foodstuff to strange people with a funny white colour. Okonta had gone on a hunting expedition in the bush when he saw a white man with a young girl. The girl was half nude, gagged and girdled with heavy chain. She was fagged out with a luggage on her head.

The white man saw Okonta and got startled at his extra-large body. He muttered a word that Okonta could not decipher. Okonta had never seen a man with such a colour in his life. He took the white man's suit and tie as extra skin and rope that was hung on the man's neck. While he made to appreciate the alien funny dressing, the white man quickly brought out a gun and depressed the trigger. It exploded in the air. Before Okonta could understand what was happening, the white man released another shot of the gun on the air. He pointed the gun at Okonta and directed him to come closer.

Okonta did not understand the white man's spoken language but acted on the sign language as he was signaled to come forward. Okonta moved close to the white man and stood aloof. He was taller and bigger than the man. But obviously the man looked more intelligent than Okonta. He quickly out smattered Okonta and commanded him to carry the luggage from the damsel.

Okonta despised the white man but signaled him to lift the luggage. "Carry it or I will kill you" the white man thundered and threatened to pull the trigger of gun. Okonta noticed the rage on the man's face and moved to lift the luggage. As Okonta bent to lift the luggage, the white quickly threw an iron net on him. Okonta blocked the net and quickly dragged the man with the net and slew him with his machete. Enraged by the white man's effort to kill him, Okonta despised and spat on his body, as it lied forlorn on his pool of blood. He chopped off the man's head and put it in his bag. He also released the damsel from the yoke that the white man placed on her.

The young girl was beautiful with full breasts, straight legs, and massive hips. Her whole body was still rich with full blood and energy that described her as a virgin. Okonta carried the white man's luggage and the girl and quickly left the bush. He entrusted the girl into Mgborie's care from the night that he brought her into the compound. Communicating with the young girl was a great problem Okonta initially had when he introduced her into the family.

She seemed to be corrupted with the white man's way of talking. With her exposure to the white man's education, she was quite alien to the language and culture of Ukpaghari people. She came from the riverside and was captured by the white man who was carrying her to the city from where she would be exported to the foreign land as a slave. Mgborie gave her the name Chika while nurturing her in the family. Okonta also adopted the name and introduced her as his third wife to the family. Okonta was always fond of Chika and he enjoined other members of the family to treat her without isolation.

It was almost seven years after Chika came

into the family and got well integrated as a legitimate wife of Okonta. She had never engaged anybody in any form of dispute in the past even though she seemed to be generally exposed than all of them. Her dispute with Mgborie was a kind of communication gap.

Sequel to Chika's grasp of the white man's education, she believed that no one man could be greater than a community no matter his strength. Mgborie had lived in Ukpaghari all through her life and she believed that no man or people could withstand Okonta or stand against his desire in the community.

While Okonta's wives were still exchanging words, he hurried into the hut. Mgborie and Ogbenyealu knelt in obeisance to welcome him, but Chika stood cold and burst into snivel lance. Okonta sat on a chair that was sandwiched by the two wives that were kneeling down and hauling encomium on him.

"You are welcome, the brave one. Your kingdom will spread through all the villages of Ukpaghari and beyond. Your strength shall multiply all the days of your life" Mgborie and Ogbenyealu praised Okonta as they were still kneeling down. He responded with a nod and remarked that something was wrong with Chika.

After Okonta acknowledged the praises from his wives, he asked them to retire to their huts we he began to interrogate Chika to find out what was her problem. Chika was still standing up and shedding tears when the other wives stepped out of the hut to their respective huts. Okonta stood up from the wooden chair he was sitting and walked to Chika who was still crying. He held her hands and began to extol her beauty and pour praises on her.

"Wipe your tears and look into my eyes," he implored. "Now tell me what your worries are," Okonta said to her while still holding her close to his body. "It is our Nnekudi; she said that I am not your legitimate wife," Chika stammered.

CHAPTER FOUR

The rooster had crowed the third time, indicating day break. Everybody got engaged in their routine activities. Numerous servants in Okonta's compound were busy sweeping the entire place while the children were in their mothers' kitchens, arranging their farm implements.

After a while, the girls carried the farming paraphernalia in baskets. They were moving to the farm with their mothers. They had to go very early to weed the farm before the sun set. Ogbenyealu usually went to the farm early and return as soon as the sun sets. Mgborie was known to stay long in the farm and seldom left the house before the third cock crow. But they were going together after the second cock crow. Chika was not going with them. She passed the night in Okonta's hut and was too weak to wake up when others were going to the farm. Ordinarily, she believed in feeding from Okonta's generosity, and usually got more than enough from Okonta instead of toiling in the farm.

Okonta had a troubling night. He was disturbed even as he was dwelling on the pleasures of Chika's beautiful body all through the night. He kept remembering the ordeal he had in the palace. His boast of being more powerful than the lords worried him. He was thinking now, how to appease the lords and get the kingship of the land.

He thought about many strategies, but a strong plan of using some members of the cabinet came to his mind. The thought lingered till morning when he woke up to face the reality of the day. He was so determined to actualize his ambition and he felt that it must be followed instantly. He was thinking about all these in his hut, with his snuff box fixed in his palm. He tapped on the snuff box and paused. He twisted the snuff box to open, then paused and began to extol the snuff before dipping his thumb on the substance and taking up a lump of the snuff into his nostril.

He paused as tears began to drip from his eyes. Okonta blinked his eyes which were absolutely red and tears dropped from it.

Then, he began to eulogize the snuff again.

"Ehhhm! Otaba; Omere nwayi Asaba; Aku nwata na agbaya anyamiri." His eyes were had turned red and he took another lump and stuffed it into his nostril. More tears enveloped his eyes and he gasped for a word.

"Who is there? He queried.

"Your servant, my lord," one of his servants hurried in. He was half naked with a piece of wrapper tied firmly on his waist. The servant was a vibrant youth that would be about twenty years of age. He looked firm, masculine, and very healthy, with his chest muscle trembling at every step, as he rushed into the hut and prostrated in obeisance. "Your servant is loyal to you my lord" he pronounced and stood up for his message.

Okonta ordered the servant to call two more servants. He had a pinch of snuff on between his fingers while talking to the servant. Before Okonta could stuff the snuff into his nostril, the servant hurried out of the hut and reappeared with other servants. Okonta ignored them and took another dose of the stuff into his nostril and sneezed noisily. He looked at the three servants that were standing before him and signaled two younger ones to go over to his right side.

He turned to the two servants that were standing at his right hand side and began to deliver the message. "Now you go to Ogbalu, that member of Itueze and tell him that I need his presence here," he said to the first servant. Then to the second person, he sent him to Ogbuefi, the member of Isieye.

"Yes my lord" the servants said simultaneously and left the hut immediately. As the boys jumped out and went for the errand, he gave the remaining one an unsympathetic look, "Come here you lazy he-goat," Okonta scolded the older servant that was standing aside, "if you are in a battle, you will be easily captured and butchered like meat by a pregnant woman. What you have learnt is that when I send you on an errand you will go and start chasing women. If you waste this time eh, only your *chi* will know what will happen to you. Now look at this," Okonta spat on the floor and charged him to return before the saliva dries up. He asked the servant to take the keg from outside and go buy a first grade palm wine from the best palm wine tapper in the village.

The compound became hushed again. Two of the Okonta's wives had gone to the farm with their children while other servants went to Okonta's farm. Okonta seldom stayed at home at this time of the day. He would either be at the farm or be engaged in one communal duty or the other. With nothing else of interest, he returned to his snuff box.

If he took one more helping of the snuff, the box would be empty. He was still contemplating what would be his next move when he saw a shadow of a human being in the compound. The shadow was coming towards the hut. Okonta never expected any person since the people had all gone out. He looked steadily at the shape of the shadow that was progressing towards his hut and was wondering who the person was.

"Who are you?" Okonta thundered as the person was at the threshold.

"Good morning my husband" Chika greeted him and bowed in obeisance. Okonta nodded and tapped on her back. Chika, who clearly looked sleepy, yawned and ambled out of the hut.

Okonta did not want her to remain in the hut after the greeting. He was not in the mood for her regular romance. He felt that such act should be done in the night. Okonta believed that romance with women should be only done in the dark of the night and behind closed doors. But Chika always drew him to romantic affairs at any time she felt like having it. This time Chika noted Okonta's mood and left him after greeting him.

All his thoughts were on the arrival of the noble men that he had invited. He was still planning on the best way to go about his plan and its consequences, when his servant that went to buy the palm wine returned.

"E hem! You came in good time. Put the wine down here" Okonta directed the servant. He requested for a cup to taste the wine. "It is a good fresh wine" he remarked after sipping the wine.

CHAPTER FIVE

Ogbalu's compound was a stone-throw distance from Okonta's compound. It was only separated by a thick bush that ran through a large portion of land. The people always avoided the bush path as they believe that an enemy could lay siege of the place and capture anybody within the area. Okonta's servant had walked past some compounds before getting to Ogbalu's compound. He saw Ogbalu and delivered the message from Okonta.

Ogbalu, like any other person in Ukpaghari had high regards for Okonta. He demonstrated this regards by sacrificing his earlier plans and started out for Okonta's compound to know why he needed him so urgently. Ogbalu was approaching the compound with a mind full of much thought. Even though they lived within the neighborhood, Okonta and Ogbalu were never used to early morning exchange of visits. He was assured that something serious must have prompted this invitation.

Okonta was expecting the guests. His servants had returned to give him assurance of their honoring the invitation. He was thinking about his plans and how to get his mission accomplished, before he heard a knock at the door.

"Come right in, whether you are a ghost or a man" Okonta remarked.

"It is me, the Ochiri Oluo of Ukpaghari" Ogbalu replied. He came in and was about to to down after a complimentary salutation with Okonta, when they heard another knock at the door. Ogbalu turned to see who was trailing him to Okonta's house.

"Who is the ghost that was following behind me?" he questioned.

"If it is a ghost, it must be a good one. Bad things never exist in my compound" Okonta said and asked the person to come in.

It was Ogbuefi, a member of Itueze. Ogbuefi was a man of great wit who always spoke in parables. He was known in the palace as a witty tortoise and he accepted the remark. Another striking feature of the man was his sense of humor which made him sensitive to anger. Immediately he stepped in and saw Ogbalu, he declared that the toad does not run in the day time for nothing. He said that something serious must have made the great warrior to seek him so urgently and decide to chase after the black goat while it is still daylight. Okonta appreciated his apt response and offered him a seat.

The three great men were still saluting each other with respect to their titles and achievements when Okonta excused himself and went into the room. He came out with a servant carrying a wooden tray of kolanuts. The servant placed the tray on a small table that was at the centre of the parlor and stepped aside. The noble men observed the traditional rites and divided the nut into four portions. Each took a piece of the kolanut remaining one for the spirit that would guide their discussion.

When noble people met, it was believed that the spirit of the ancestors must be present to bless their discussions. And the portion of the kolanut that was left was for the spirit of the ancestors. This spirit could come in the form of unanticipated guest. As they were eating the kolanut, Okonta directed his servant to bring the keg of wine. The servant quickly brought the wine and fetched some cups of animal horns. Okonta took one of the cups and collected a little quantity of the wine and drank before the guests. "This is your wine" Okonta announced to the guests.

"Great lion, hope you did not mean to spoil us with delicacies this early hour of the day?" Ogbalu remarked to the amazement of the noble men.

The parlour became lively and the people drank and merry with rambunctious laughter. They seemed to forget the gist of their gathering as they were enjoying the fresh palm wine from the best wine tapper in the village. Okonta wanted it that way. He wanted them to be relaxed and discuss without restrictions.

"Please fill my cup once more," Ogbalu

requested.

"Great one, please enjoy yourself nobody knows whether there would be good palm wine tappers in our next world" Ogbuefi said jokingly. "But we have been drinking without an inkling of why the great lion of Ukpaghari summoned us this early hour of the day" He called the attention of the people to the gist of their gathering, saying that they needed to discuss before being drunk.

"You are right wise one," Ogbalu commented. He was half drunk and it showed in his face as he looked dazed. He had been drinking like a loafer and wanted to continue drinking before Ogbuefi called them to order. But he managed to withhold the urge for more and affirmed to Ogbuefi's request that they hear from Okonta.

Okonta had been looking for an opportunity to break the substance of the gathering until Ogbuefi made the request. He quickly gulped a chunk of the drink and paused. His expression changed as he looked at the men and began to speak.

"Noble men of Ukpaghari, it is the matter of our great kingdom that called for this gathering this moment." He paused and regarded the two men who were very quiet. None of them uttered a word, but seemingly expected to hear more of the words. Okonta observed their feelings and continued to extol the kingdom. He recounted the various achievements of the land and how their neighbors made efforts to conquer their forefathers, but by the efforts of their warriors, the people failed. He remembered how their late king led the warriors to fight against some warriors from other lands and came back victorious.

"Now tell me who will lead our warriors to war in case of any invasion of our land by enemies, especially now that we don't have a king" He did not wait for them to answer the question before he continued, "I don't think that our ancestors who established the kingship were foolish to have done so. They knew the significance before establishing the stool and we cannot abolish it in this generation," Okonta said and told Ogbuefi and Ogbalu that he needed them to make their colleagues in Itueze and Isieye to support his course of becoming the great king of Ukpaghari.

"Please convince them to crown me as the Ukpa of Ukpaghari" he concluded.

He proposed strategies of getting the people to reason with them. Okonta further proposed the idea of the two prominent members of the king makers to invite majority of the members to their houses. "The people should be invited for a dinner individually and let it be that they converged informally and you will discuss the matter in such a gathering.

The men listened with rapt attention as Okonta declared the strategies of getting the kingmakers into his course of getting the throne. He had never been all that serious except there was rumor of war. He was actually making sense to the people.

Okonta noted the facial expression of the noble men and got convinced that his course was in progress, enjoined them to hold the meeting with the selected people before the next joint meeting of the two houses of the kingmakers. The Isieye would hold their separate meeting in the next "Nkwor" market day while the "Itueze" would hold theirs a day after the "Nkwor" market day. Okonta targeted at getting some cohorts before the joint meeting to enable him get reasonable support in the meeting.

He promised powerful positions to the collaborators. He promised to appoint the noble men as leaders of their groups if they would support his course for the throne. The message was received with mixed feelings of both optimism and doubt. Okonta's power was not in doubt. They knew that since he was resolute about arrogating the throne to himself, there may not be any impediment. But their doubt was on the tradition. "Ehmm, you know…" Ogbalu was about uttering some words when Okonta interrupted him.

"Yes, I am aware of what it takes to host such

noble members of your groups. As you know very well, I never sleep over relevant matters. I am well prepared for the meetings" Okonta declared and quickly went into the room. The two men remained cold, watching things as they were unfolding.

After a while, Ogbalu broke the silence.

"What can you say about this?" He asked Ogbuefi

"My opinion is as good as yours" Ogbuefi replied and continued. "But, ehm…" he was crossing his arms, nodding in affirmation of the plans.

"I am equally in support of the course" Ogbalu said. They became a little bit more curious, and it showed in their faces as they expressed the solidarity with Okonta.

Okonta quickly returned to the parlour. He became amazed at the effect of his action and could not avoid the smile that was beaming on his face. "This is how my kingdom would be, full of joy and understanding" He said in appreciation of the cordiality between his new collaborators.

Okonta was carrying some bags of coins. The coin was a new way of payment in the land. It was invented by the white man. Before this time, nobody used the coins except for jewelry. The only means of exchange was trade by barter. If you have yam and needed maize, the quantity you put for exchange will determine the quantity you will receive. The trade by barter system was taken over by coins after the white man's invasion of the land. Okonta had enough of it as evidence of his hard works. And he was ready to lavish a chunk of the coins to get the throne. He counted the coins and gave a bag of it each to the noble men. "Use this to buy snuff and prepare sumptuous dinner for the people that would be invited in your house," he said to each of the men.

CHAPTER SIX

Ukpaghari was such a homogenous kingdom that was integrated by many things from common ancestors to their architectural designs. They had a foundation of communalism that was bequeathed to them from the creation of the world. No member of the community can cause the blood of another person in the kingdom. It was believed that a fire that was kindled in one kitchen will illuminate the entire kingdom. Their houses were clustered in the nucleus of the kingdom while their farm lands were in distant virgin lands.

Women return from the farm

Women and weaker men farm within the residential areas while the strong ones farm in faraway lands. Most of the distant farms were located at the borders with neighboring communities. It was believed that the distant farms lands were more fertile than those within the residential areas. However, going to the distant farms looked like making a journey outside the community. It would be tortuous, hectic and risky. Most people leave their houses in the morning and on their way to the farm encounter head hunters in expedition or roving ghost who could kidnap them and take them to the spirit world. Elders used to tell the young ones about a story of a belle who was going to the distant farm unaccompanied by an elder and she met a wicked ghost who stole her beauty and bequeathed her with great ugliness.

The road looked frightening with big trees, wild animals and shrills from various birds piercing the serenity of the path. Nobody could dare go to the farm alone. They moved in groups.

Okonta's wives, Mgborie and Ogbenyealu were going with members of other families within the neighborhood. They were jovial as they discussed recent events in the community. While people from Okonta's family were making efforts to direct the discussion to events, other people in the group were keen on discussing Okonta's bid for the throne. It was actually the paramount issue in the community.

Two women in the group were very garrulous in the discussion.

"I don't know what the world has turned to," the first woman remarked.

"I have been lost in thought why Okonta-nwa-Otamba should be threatening to kill all our palace leaders for denying him the throne" she said.

"Oh, should that be why Onyema was calling a meeting of opinion leaders in the next Eke day?" The second woman asked.

They discussed the matter but held back their opinion against Okonta's quest for the throne.

It was getting late as the sun was already peeping through the sky. It was rapidly becoming bright and forcing the sun to shine on late comers to the farm. Any person that went to the farm when the sun had started shining would be considered a lazy farmer. This made the farmers hasten up on their way to the farm.

In accordance with the tradition of the community, farm lands were not individually owned; they were usually shared to lineages, compounds, and families. They believed that the method would help in creating the friendliness that was prevalent in the community. Everybody had his or her relation within the boundaries of his or her farmland. On that note, the issue of Okonta's quest was the subject of discussion by families and lineages while resting in the farm.

Everyone knew about Okonta's intention but with divergent views. However, members of the community believed that everything would end at the next Isieye and Itueze meeting. Outcome of the meeting would decide the popular candidate to the throne. If Okonta would come out victorious at the meeting, it would be a revolutionary movement. But on the contrary, tradition would remain supreme.

Okonta's cronies had been diligently planning to enthrone him in the next meeting of the Palace Cabinet. Ogbuefi had convened some members of Isieye to a dinner in his compound. He carefully did the invitation so that the people would not preempt his motive for the meeting. It was to look like any other gathering of friends at the end of every farming exercise in the community. Ordinarily, the village square used to be very boisterous every evening with rambunctious chatting predicated on hot arguments. Also, they used to gather at the square to get a gist of events in the community.

It was in one of the evening gatherings that the elders got information about the visitation of men with funny and pitiable colours in their skins. They were called 'White man' because of their skin colour that was unfortunately white. The purveyor of the information of the 'White man' said that they were talking through their nose like people that had serious catarrh, and only the gods could decipher their language.

Ogbuefi used to be loud and always came up with superior opinions in the village square discussions. He exploited this advantage as he went to those people that used to cluster at the square and invited them to his house. They were mostly members of the Isieye. His ability to sell the idea to them would be able to convince the entire house. This group was always fond of each other, and often shares dinner at each other's benevolence. But it goes without invitation.

Eating together was another form of gregarious culture of the ranks and file of the community.

CHAPTER SEVEN

Ogbuefi knew that time spent with his friends would be sacrificed for his goals. He had that at heart as the dinner was going on. It was a very delicious pottage that was served in large quantity. No one pot could carry the quantity of food that served to the men. One seeing the heap of food served would believe that the men would rarely consume the entire food. Actually, they had the meal and lapsed into a food-stupor.

While they were eating, Akpaka, a very vibrant and talkative fellow among the friends queried the source of Ogbuefi's effusive benevolence. Ogbuefi surveyed the men and observed the curiosity in their faces. He pushed another piece of the potage into his mouth and mumbled. What he said was not audible.

He called for palm wine to the utmost surprise of his friends. It was like the servants were already waiting with the wine. Immediately, they appeared with two kegs of palm wine. Also, two of his wives brought an additional cooked pot of the pottage to complement the wine. They quickly emptied the additional food in the clay pot from where they scooped the food to their individual plates.

The servants were still waiting with the kegs of palm wine when Ogbuefi told them to drop the wine and leave immediately. He made sure that every one of them enjoyed the food and drank the palm wine before he sighed and made a remark that attracted the attention to him. "Wonderful things are happening these days," he had said.

"What is the issue this time" Unara asked

"It is all about a rat that wants to wage a war with an elephant."

"Who is the rat?" Ndubuisi queried.

"It is 'nwa nza' that is trying its god"

"Talk to your friends in a clear language" Akpaka voiced.

"Have you forgotten that a child who begs for interpretation of proverb is wasting his mother's bride price?" Ogbuefi remarked jokingly.

There were different remarks by members of the group which caused a lively noise in the compound. They insisted on the interpretation of the proverb. Ogbuefi laughed mockingly at them, accusing the noble men of denouncing their birth right for a piece of information that is momentary.

"Well" he continued, "it is all about our small neighbor at the west bank of Otenzu River"

"You mean the Amankalu people?" Ndubuisi asked.

"Exactly my dear, they are on their course again.

"Which course, if I may ask?" Echeme asked. Ogbuefi felt sad about the question.

"Why do you ask such question, are you the only one in the river who does not know the root of the fish? Ogbuefi quipped and continued. "Amankalu people had fought for our lands during the reign of Ikpeoha, but for the brave intervention of great warriors like Okonta, their efforts would have been a success. Now two days ago, as I was going to buy some snuff from Amankwo junction, I heard from one market woman who was discussing with her friend, that in a few days from now, the warriors of Amankalu would invade our market to kidnap our women with a ransom of the piece of land they fought for during the reign of Ikpeoha. As I heard that, I became terrified. I made effort to identify the woman so that I could make further enquiry on the issue, but she was a very strange fellow that I could not identify her.

The men were awed by the story that they allowed tranquillity to prevail for a while. They were only nodding their heads in affirmation of the story. They became temporarily dumb before Unara defiled the situation with a remark. "Well, we shall trash them as usual,"

But before he could round off the statement, Orji snapped in, "Remember that we do not have a king as at now to command our warriors to go into war, if we should be ready for any war we had better crown our king immediately."

"Who is the heir apparent, Ukpandu or Okonta? Ndubuisi asked.

"I prefer Okonta to Ukpandu in a situation like the one our friend has narrated. Ukpandu cannot command warriors like Okonta in a war situation. Unara posited.

"Incredible! How would a man, in his right senses think of crowning another person for what does not belong to him?" Ndubuisi exclaimed.

"It is impossible" Echeme affirmed.

Ogbuefi observed the divergent views and quickly intervened. He had created the desired atmosphere for his course. He made good use of it as he remarked in a very high tone. "It is possible" he exclaimed.

"Yes it is. When a drum sounds hot, the dancers should follow the tune. At least, the situation calls for it. Now tell me, which is more important; our tradition or our community? Shall we protect our tradition to the detriment of the community? What would posterity hold about our generation; what shall we bequeath the future generations with if people from other communities would invade us and seize our land? Our elders said that when a king is strong, his people would equally be strong." He paused and probed the audience. He was expecting them to be decisive on selecting Okonta against the heir apparent. Without them making overt assertion toward that, he was convinced that the men had been convinced and would definitely support the selection of Okonta-nwa-Otamba as the King of

Ukpaghari but the herculean task was how to convince the enlarged house into supporting the course. However, they finally agreed to present Okonta before the Isieyes to be crowned in the next meeting.

It was getting dark; the sun had really gone beneath the sky allowing the shadows to still across the sky. The noble men had eating to satisfaction. Ogbuefi was equally satisfied that his aim of convincing the noble men was achieved. He further gratified the men with portions of tobacco stuffed in their boxes.

In appreciation of the Ogbuefi's effusive benevolence, Orji remarked "Our elders have said that if nakedness promises you a clothing item, ask his source. So my noble friend if you wouldn't mind, may I ask the source of this generosity?"

Ogbuefi ignored him and stuffed a pinch of the snuff into his nostril. He gasped momentarily as his eyes that were beclouded by tears turned red. It was like the snuff obstructed his nose and he managed to breathe through his mouth. With his mouth open gasping for breath, he struggled to reply to Orji's remark.

"You know that an animal that does not have a tail depends on its god to chase away flies that perch on its body. If you think that wealth was not weighty enough to carry my benevolence to august friends like you and others, my 'chi' had provided for me.

"Gbam," other friends chorused in affirmation as they began to take and share the snuff in turns.

People of Ukpaghari live in each other's benefits. Whoever was blessed by his 'chi' would never hesitate to share what he has with others. They believed in their neighbours as they could believe in themselves. That was why the noble men did not drag the source of Ogbuefi's benevolence too long and took share of the snuff.

CHAPTER EIGHT

Ogbalu was an average man in terms of wealth acquisition. He was neither too rich nor poor by any standard. He had a beautiful compound, numerous wives and children. Ogbalu was popular for maintaining an outstanding happy family where everybody lived happily with each other. One hardly distinguished the children borne by the wives. Also, his modesty distinguished him from his peers. He would greet everybody old and young, rich and poor without reservation.

His contemporaries identified him with beautiful and amiable women, and he had a good number of them among his seven wives. Ogbalu loved all in the Kingdom except the *'efulefu'* who drink to stupor in public functions. He was known to be prompt to functions and would never stay any longer than the end of the event before returning to his compound.

Ogbalu was also known as a great thinker. To him, what makes a man was his ability to think positively. His philosophy was that a man was dead as soon as he stopped thinking. He often asserted in every discussion that God gave people head for various reasons. Some people have their heads only to carry loads while others have theirs for thinking. He belonged to the class of people who used their heads for thinking. He would never give immediate answer to any question without thinking over it. As a result of this, Ogbalu seldom had time for frivolity and gatherings for mere merry making.

In contrast to his attribute, Ogbalu was eating and drinking with a good number of Ituezes in his compound. They were selected on their individual capacities, and only the invited members were there. Those invited were Elezuo, Igwo, Urum, and Olere with himself as the host. Each of them had a bowl of sumptuous pounded yam foofoo with kegs of palm wine to digest the food.

It was at the early hour of the night, beams of light from the various kitchens surrounding the compound chased away shadows of darkness in the compound. The place was highly illuminated and the presence of the beautiful wives of Ogbalu made it look subtle and bloom. The women were putting on cheerful and elegant postures that tickled the fancy of lechers among the group.

Ogbalu's friends drinking in his compound

The men were so lively while enjoying the food with jokes that made the place very loving and desiring. Igwo swallowed a lump of the pounded yam and smiled radiantly. He caressed his pot belly that had protruded like that of a pregnant woman, he teased Ogbalu, "I have seen why our friend Ogbalu was always coming late to meetings."

"Why, is it because of his beautiful wives?" Elezuo queried.

"No, not at all, but because of the sumptuous

dishes they serve at his table," Urum uttered.

Ogbalu seemed not to like the joke. He was in deep thought as he gulped his drink and waved his hand disapprovingly of what the men uttered.

"If life ends at sweet dishes, I would be free from problems" Ogbalu declared and took a sip of palm wine.

"What then would be the matter that troubles our friend that we don't know?" Olere queried

"Our community of course; especially now that we don't have a king, we are like a horde of sheep without a shepherd," he quipped.

"Ukpandu would soon be crowned the King of Ukpaghari," Elezuo suggested.

"That was why I am troubled about our community," Ogbalu continued.

"What is more problematic than this? Ukpandu is a woman. And a woman cannot rule a land like the great Ukpaghari," he posited.

The people looked bemused as they remained calm and focused on Ogbalu who was seriously grieved in his tone. Their lips went dry with bewilderment. Igwo dragged his buttocks on the wooden chair he was sitting on, but his pot belly seemed uncomfortable as he bent towards Ogbalu to get the gist of the matter.

Urum was nodding in affirmative of all that Ogbalu was saying. He face was beaming with admiration of Ogbalu's words, whereas other members still maintained the confusion in their countenances. Ogbalu noticed the support that Urum was giving and leveraged it to stimulate others into agreeing with him.

As soon as Ogbalu rounded off his words, Urum quickly suggested that they would champion the course of enthroning Okonta as the next King of Ukpaghari. They agreed with Ogbalu and Urum that Okonta had the qualities of a King of Ukpaghari, but that the tradition forbade the revolutionary charisma presented by Okonta. Urum further called attention of the group to the fact that Okonta was more of a King than Ukpandu, but for the sake of the tradition, the throne may elude Okonta.

Ogbalu agreed with Urum but frowned at the statement that the throne may elude Okonta. Ogbalu asked, "Protection of the Kingdom versus upholding the tradition bequeathed on us by our fathers, which one is more important?" He paused and looked sideways at the people.

Olere quickly answered, "Although tradition is a legacy, it is when the place is protected that you would be alive to observe the tradition."

Each member of the group was careful about his utterance. They left Ogbalu to do more of the talking while they listened and answered questions. This made Ogbalu to change from calm disposition to eloquent personality.

"We don't need a seer to tell us that we need to choose somebody who can protect us as a king.

After all, tradition is an inherited pattern of thought which may be altered by the dynamic nature of life. Tradition is only started by a generation and posterity nurtures it." As he spoke along, he further posited that the prevailing situation of the Kingdom demanded urgent alteration of the tradition for the survival of the kingdom.

Urum supported him by declaring that revolution creates history, and that they should champion the revolution without hesitation. In a snappy thunderous tone, Ogbalu snatched the word from Urum saying,

"If one's god puts salt in his mouth and he says that it is bitter; it would be immediately removed from his mouth. Now that our god had created the revolution ideas into our minds, we don't need to kill it, else posterity will not forgive us when our kingdom would be defeated by neighbors."

He urged the people to champion the revolution immediately. There was an air of calmness before Olere greeted and called on them to agree with Ogbalu without hesitation.

It was already night, darkness had taken oven the sky. But the people did not notice the atmosphere as they continued pondering on the prevailing matter. At the end of the discussion, they agreed that Okonta-nwa-Otamba would be crowned and that they would vehemently oppose contrary view at the next Isieye meeting.

CHAPTER NINE

Many families had taken their dinner and restricted their movements to their compounds. Children had gone to their mothers' kitchens listening to folk tales from elders. These tales were talked about common people. Some of them were animal tales, dilemma tales, ghost stories, and foundation stories. They were used to build in to the subconscious of the younger generations, the values and morals of society which they were made to internalize.

The weather was cold and fire was ignited in various kitchens where these tales were being told, to warm up the place. Babies were sitting in their mother's laps and most times wrapped well against catching cold.

Outside the kitchen, nothing was moving. It was as if the ghosts were meeting. The wind was blowing roughly, provoking the branches of trees to send protesting sound. It was as if a heavy rain would fall. This scared children from having their usual moonlight play. Ordinarily, when mostly girls listen to folktales in their mother's kitchens, boys and some stubborn girls usually engage in moonlight play within the compound or in the square.

All domestic animals had gone into their habitations. Any rooster that crows at this time of the night would portend danger in the land. The quietness of the time would enable the crier to disseminate information to the community. The town crier was the chief information officer of the community. He had the sanctimonious air while discharging his duties, no one was allowed to talk to him or greet him in order to free him from possible disturbance while on duty.

The town crier was beating the drum "kpom! Kpom! Kpom!" yelling a sound that synchronized with the percussive instrument to make the night grow colder. "Yoohoooo!" he yelled while beating the drum three times. Shrilling insects were thrilled to calmness and abrupt tranquility beclouded the atmosphere. "Ehm, my lords and good people of Ukpaghari, please listen attentively," the town crier continued. "I greet you all" "Kpom" he beat the drum again and continued. "This message is for the lords of the land. There will be an important combined meeting of the Ituezes and Isieyes in the next Nkwor market day. Any member of the bodies that fails to attend the meeting shall forfeit his membership" Kpom! Kpom!! He beat the drum again before concluding the announcement. "He who hears should tell his neighbour." Kpom! Kpom!! Kpom!!! He beat the drum three times to sign off after disseminating the message. He went on around the entire Ukpaghari community.

CHAPTER TEN

Meetings of Ituezes and Ituezes had taken place preceding the combined meeting of the two bodies. Both meetings did not end with common interest of members. Ogbalu and Ogbuefi had made effort to persuade the two bodies into adopting Okonta as the consensus heir to the throne, but the conservatives among them insisted on crowning the heir apparent. However, majority of the membership of the two bodies were convinced by Ogbalu and Ogbuefi respectively.

The night had been far spent and all lights had gone off. It was the time that ghosts moved around the place. All mortals had gone to sleep after the day's activities. Okonta was still awake in the night. He was overwhelmed by thoughts of the Kingship. He had never had peace since the town crier's announcement. Neither Ogbalu nor Ogbuefi had met with him to give him a feedback of their various meetings. These gave him worries that he could not sleep. The combined meeting would take place the following day where the selection of the king would be made before the public coronation.

Outside the room was darkness that signaled the meeting of ghosts at every nook and cranny of the land. Hooting of the owl was echoing in the dark. Owl was a bird of the night which was believed to herald the presence of the dead to the land the living. When the owl hoots, it means that something dangerous was going to happen. It was at this precarious condition of the night that Okonta's servants went knocking at the doors of Ogbalu and Ogbuefi respectively.

Okonta was much tensed as he was waiting for the arrival of the noble men. Any delay in the arrival culminated to his horror. He could neither sit down nor stand up in the parlor. He quickly jerked the door to move out of the parlor. The place was too dark that he could not see even a white object situated within a short range. It was also deadly silent and cold, but it was like a crowd of people were marching on his head and his nerves could not contend with the heat that was oozing out of his body.

He was talking to himself when he heard an unclear foot sound. Okonta became more curious when the sound was drawing closer; he made a brisk movement towards the source of the sound.

His nerves were responding to the impulse of the sound as he was moving towards the foot sound. Suddenly, he started hearing another foot sound coming from his back. The sound started coming from every direction, even as the hooting of the owl was echoing harshly.

Okonta had poised for a fight with the spirit when the sound abruptly stopped. The tranquility returned to the place with a low male voice beckoning Okonta. "What is the matter that would keep the King out of the comfort of his beautiful wives at this time of the night?” Ogbuefi queried the presence of Okonta outside his room in the night. Okonta heaved a sigh of relief and held his hand without saying a word. His servant who returned with Ogbuefi bowed and went into the house as Ogbuefi and Okonta were also walking into the house.

They were at the door post when Ogbalu arrived with the servant that went to call him.

“May your days be long, the great King of Ukpaghari” Ogbalu greeted.

“Thank you the noble one” Okonta responded and offered a hand shake with him.

They embraced each other and walked into the parlour. The house was dark; all the lights had been put off before members of the family went to sleep. But being familiar with the parlour, Ogbalu and Ogbuefi were able to locate were the chairs were as they got seated and Okonta quickly went into the room.

Okonta returned to the parlour with a burning stick of wax that illuminated the place. He also had a wooden tray containing kolanut and alligator pepper. He placed the burning wax on a stand and passed the kolanut to Ogbuefi.

“I am suggesting that the kolanut would go with the night as we skip it to go straight into our reason of gathering this night when others were deep at sleep. Ogbuefi quipped while holding the kolanut tray offered by Okonta.

"I beg to disagree with you, this kolanut is from the King and it cannot be rejected at any time of the day or night. Ogbalu objected and urged Ogbuefi to go on with the ritual of kolanut presentation.

"Thank you my noblemen, I called you to know all about the snakes we collectively killed" Okonta said to the people.

"Yes, I met with members of Ituezes and they have agreed to crown Okonta as the new King in the joint meeting that would hold tomorrow. Ogbalu explained.

"And the Isieyes are with us," Ogbuefi chipped in. "This is good news my noble one. Is it the entire Isieye or your selected members did the agreement to crown me?" Okonta asked Ogbuefi. "Well my group is the majority" Ogbuefi quickly answered.

Okonta's face beamed with smile as he lifted a bottle of gin and called for celebration.

"Now I can proudly beat my chest as the incoming King of Ukpaghari. Then you Ogbuefi would be the leader of Isieye and Ogbalu would become the leader of Ituezes," Okonta declared.

Okonta pouring libation

He poured some contents of the gin into a cup and began to pour libation saying, "Kamalu, the god of thunder; Agwunsi, the god of vengeance. We greet you all. The gods of our great ancestors; the gods of our land, we greet you all."

"Iseeeh" The men chorused in response.

Okonta continued after a momentary silence;

"Birds of the night; the wind blows in the night, we know that you are listening to our message."

"Iseeeh!" The men responded as Okonta continued.

"The walls of this building; the land that we are standing on; we crave your ears to our discussion."

"Iseeeh!"

Okonta paused, and regarded the men with the cup of gin in his hand and continued, "It is the love of our land Ukpaghari that prompted our collaboration and seek your support to this quest for the stool of Ukpaghari Kingship. We know that you are with us. Any person that rises against this mission, may Kamalu the god never see the person well."

"Iseeeh" The men responded.

"Whatever that will bring impediment to the achievement of the mission, may the wind of the night blow it away."

"Iseeeh" The men responded

"Lead us well to lead the people aright. This is our request which must come to pass."

"Iseeeehhh" The men chorused.

Okonta poured the last drop of the gin on the floor to appease the gods and poured another quantity on the cup and gulped it.

He was welcomed back from the gods by Ogbalu and Ogbuefi. "Thank you the noble ones, the gods are in support of our mission" Okonta noted while gulping another drop of the gin.

They went into discussion on how to enthrone without delay. Ogbalu advised Okonta to present himself humbler than ever because they will surely crown him even if other members of the house opposed to it. Okonta nodded in appreciation.

Ogbuefi said, "Immediately the orator calls the meeting to order, I will propose the crowning of the king. My men will support me and I will pronounce Okonta as the man to be crowned. After this nomination, you Ogbalu will ask your members to crown him without delay." The idea was welcomed by the people but Okonta reminded them that the festival of the seventh month was almost at hand when he would come out to address the masses.

"We better go now before the day breaks; it seems the moon was angry with the sky as it refused to show up. Ogbuefi quipped and they dispersed.

CHAPTER ELEVEN

Okonta opened the snuff box and fed his nostrils lavishly with the stuff. He paused and cleared the nostrils by blowing it, took another generous dose into his nostrils and gasped for breath.

His compound had become lively once again. The servants were at their duty posts, cleaning the compound and other chores.

He was sitting in the parlour where his wives were in turn coming to prostrate in obeisance, pouring praises on their hero. Okonta regarded each of the women with great affection as they were kneeling before him. He later called his wives together and instructed them not to go to the farm, but rather to stay at home to welcome the noble men that would accompany him home after the coronation at the meeting of king makers. He also requested them to prepare sumptuous meal for the august visitors.

The compound was in a festive mood. Everybody in the compound was very happy and cheerfully expressing delight on the expected victory of Okonta at the meeting. In the spirit of the acquired royal blood into the family, Mgborie and Ogbenyealu separately prepared delicious pounded yam and cassava breakfast for the entire family. Okonta ate to his satisfaction and quickly got ready for the meeting.

The morning was still virgin. It was a bright

one as the sun was rising from its sleep. The clement weather made the community lively as the people were going about their endeavours in the farm. Members of the palace were going to the palace for the very important meeting of the joint ruling bodies of the palace. They seldom met in this manner except for an important discussion like the one of today.

Before the sun set, all and sundry in the palace had been seated. The clan rulers who were like observers were equally seated at the gallery while the Ituezes and Isieyes were seated at the podium.

Iwuoha the chief orator stood up to call the meeting to order.

"Great leaders of the land, you are welcome to the palace. Whenever the palace is filled with all the honorable and reputable people of our land, the palace and its rank and file would rejoice. The dog has said, that it follows a potbellied man because he would surely either excrete something, or vomit something. We know that an august meeting like this would definitely benefit the kingdom in many ways. We are sure that something great would definitely emanate from this gathering."

The crowd listened as he spoke.

"However, this gathering means more than anything great for the community. This is the sixth month of the year; the next month will be the seventh month when the next king of Ukpaghari will come to the public. Since the death of our great king Ikpeoha, we have spent many months without a king. This is to the detriment of the kingdom."

Everyone was paying attention to every word he uttered.

"On this note, we had agreed that the king will be crowned in this month in anticipation of the public presentation in the festival of the seventh month. We are today to crown the king so that he will come to the public in the next month. According to our tradition, the Isieye will propose the king while the Ituezes would crown him. Therefore, we shall give Ichie Oyia this period to meet briefly with the members of Isieyes and propose the king of Ukpaghari for the coronation." Iwuoha looked around the people, rounded off his speech and said, "I greet you once again my Lords," before returning to his seat a the middle of the pavilion.

The joint meeting was a traditional ceremony for the presentation and coronation of the king. Before the joint meeting the Isieyes usually hold their exclusive meeting where they agree on the candidate that would be presented at the joint meeting.

However, the last meeting of the Isieyes ended in chaos, but the majority of the members insisted on Okonta being presented at the joint meeting. The brief meeting could not make a difference as the Isieyes were reluctantly returning to their chamber for the formal presentation of the king.

The Isieyes' court of the palace was a small room designed for their meetings. Each member had his stool in the court. Any erring member of the Isieye would be punished by having his stool removed from the court. That would be a severe punishment.

Oyia's stool was conspicuously situated with his subordinates. He quickly got seated for the meeting at the court. Though they were all wearing gruesome faces but managed to hold the meeting as Oyia called the meeting to other.

Ogbuefi remained calm and moody. His mind was full of grief. More to it was when Oyia faked a smile to appease the troubled minds of members. Still in the mood of depression, Ogbuefi stood and craved the attention of the people. "Our Kingdom needs a new king; we must find him and present him for coronation. Let us go at it immediately and present him before the palace would become tired of waiting," Ogbuefi said to the Isieyes.

"Don't jump over issues. We should at least commence the meeting before opinions would be gathered," Oyia cautioned.

"Let us present Okonta-nwa-Otamba as we had agreed before now" Unara retorted.

There was uproar in the chamber as everybody started talking at the same time. Some of them were talking in support of Okonta while others were vehemently against such suggestion.

"Ukpandu is the heir apparent, our tradition made it clear that the heir should be crowned after the death of the father" Oyia insisted, arguing that the tradition must be upheld.

"Ukpaghari which is a land of great warriors cannot be ruled by a man who is more less a woman," Ogbuefi and his cohorts insisted. There were hot debates as Ogbuefi's group became aggressive and maintained that Okonta must be presented for coronation.

At the end Oyia resolved to go by the majority, for more than half of the Isieyes stood for Okonta. "This is a rape of our tradition," Oyia exclaimed and decided to renegade on the traditional duty of presenting heir to the throne. Ogbuefi who was at the background championing the course of events, burst out laughing as Oyia decided to relinquish his position than to present someone other than the rightful heir to the throne.

"Coward begets coward. Indeed he is not capable of presenting the great warrior Okonta to the palace. But I, a stronger person in all ramifications can do so without fear of any consequence. After all, we are taking a stand for the security of our kingdom," Ogbuefi said with a standing ovation from the members.

With great amazement, Ndubuisi called for the presentation of Okonta before the Isieyes prior to formal presentation to the palace. There was a lingering uproar as many were still applauding Ogbuefi's bravery in taking up the challenge of presenting Okonta. He had led a foundation for revolution in the kingdom. Oyia and other conservatives were terribly aggrieved by the development.

Ndubuisi had already gone to bring in Okonta without the approval of the leader. He returned with Okonta following him into the chamber of the Isieye. Okonta was now relaxed unlike his first appearance when he only exhibited a confrontational temper. His face was radiating joy and pride as he walked in shoulder high into the chamber. The Isieyes in turn began to pour encomium on him. Okonta greeted the members and took a seat that was reserved for him.

Oyia who was rigid in the battle of upholding the tradition quickly moved out of the chamber as Okonta got seated, thus moving back the defeated Ukpandu, the son of the late King.

"Lords of the land, I wouldn't be such a coward that would watch the tradition of our land being raped in broad day light. I insist that the legitimate heir to the throne be presented to the palace, and he is here standing with me." Before Oyia could say the last word, the people began to boo him, calling him names in a total disregard of

Ukpandu's presence.

Ukpandu was standing like a loafer in the midst of the noblemen. His feet were not strong on the ground. It was like he was intimidated by the presence of Okonta and the noblemen. His tall slim physique made him look like he would be swept out of the ground by any slight wind. With his voice sounding as if he wanted to cry, Ukpandu greeted the house and made to talk but was not given the privilege of talking in the house.

Ogbuefi noticed the agony in Ukpandu's tone and gave him a mocking recognition while requesting that he should be allowed to say what he had in mind. Okonta who was already prepared to move with the Isieyes to the palace waited to listen to Ukpandu's words. Ogbuefi gave another contemptuous look on Oyia and Ukpandu who was gasping for word.

"Our land has not degenerated to the extent of having a pauper as the leader. We cannot afford to lose the Kingdom because of tradition. We have chosen Okonta and we are presenting him to the palace," Ogbuefi remarked as Ukpandu stood in bewilderment.

"Oyia, are you not ashamed of presenting this woman for coronation? You want this man that was chased out his hut by a hen to your king? Alright, go ahead and present him," Ndubuisi mocked Oyia's effort on insisting on the coronation of Ukpandu.

It was like Ukpandu was pushed to the wall as other members of Isieye threw more insults at him. Hatred, fear and agony showed on his face. He was pinched where it hurt most. But he repelled the feeling and made to stand tall in his remark.

"Great men of Isieye, I salute your decision, but our elders said that when death knocks on the door of a dog, it would not allow it to perceive the smell of faeces. The same elders also said that the tallest tree sees farther than the others. Oyia, by virtue of his position, knows the consequence of your choice. Therefore, I enjoin you to give up and uphold the tradition of the land because; I am the legitimate heir to the throne."

Okonta moved to destroy Ukpandu

Before Ukpandu could finish all he wanted to say, Okonta sprang from the seat like a lion about to catch a prey. He gnashed his teeth and roared in anger.

"Shut up your mouth! Who taught you to talk? Say a word again and watch me pluck your feather since you think you can now fly," Okonta thundered as he rushed to grab Ukpandu, but members of Isieyes held him back.

Okonta was breathing heavily. His muscles were charged to pounce and demolish Ukpandu.

He believed that a breath spent on talking with Ukpandu was a wasted one. He would rather tear him to shreds than waste his breath on talking to him. He really meant to tear Ukpandu down, but the members of Isieye knew he would do it, and so they held him back, trying to calm his nerves. He however, was able to overcome all the efforts of the Isieyes and grabbed Ukpandu by his neck, squeezing hard to strangulate him.

Ukpandu was already suffocating before Ogbuefi intervened. "Okonta-nwa-Otamba, please leave this woman before you commit murder."

Other members joined in appealing to Okonta to let go of Ukpandu's neck. He gave Ukpandu a severe steady look before he allowed his half dead body to slump to the ground.

Now, the Isieyes represent the entire people of Ukpaghari. They are selected by the large families of the Kingdom. Any family that was not represented at the Isieye was like the family was ostracized. That was why their choice of a king is inviolable. Members of Itueze were chosen elders that ratify and pronounce decisions of the Isieyes.

Flanked by the group of Isieyes, Ogbuefi was beaming with joy as he presented Okonta-nwa-Otamba as the consensus choice of the masses as represented by the Isieyes. He was doing that with his mouth wide open in pride. He saluted the palace after the presentation of Okonta for coronation.

"You are welcome, the great people of our land. The King makers have been waiting to hear from you. Ehhm!" Okechi paused, cleared his throat and continued. "According to our tradition it is the leader of Isieyes representing the entire house before the king makers. We would first like to know why this abnormality?" Okechi, the leader of Itueze was known as an ardent custodian of tradition. He was also known for his prudence, conservative approach to issues, and would rather forfeit every benefit than be a party to an abnormality.

Okechi was carefully observing the happenings as Ogbuefi was presenting Okonta for coronation instead of Oyia making the presentation. He was pondering over the consequence and asking questions about the leader of the Isieye when Ogbalu interrupted aggressively to the amazement of all in the palace.

"Is it their leader or the heir that we are going to crown? We better crown the person presented by the Isieye immediately" Ogbalu snapped.

Infuriated by the rude interruption, Okechi gave a stern look at Ogbalu and cautioned. "Don't jump at issues because they at times determine your faith," he said to Ogbalu.

The presence of Okonta and Ogbuefi raised some dust among the Ituezes. There was a sharp division among the king makers. The conservatives saw what was happening as an aberration while others saw it as a necessary revolution for the interest of the kingdom. However, Okechi was very resolute on defending the tradition.

While the struggle for the stool was rising to a dangerous crescendo, Ogbuefi abruptly interrupted in a loud voice. "My lords, let my presence not be a cause of discord among the noble men of Itueze. Our leader, Oyia felt sick and was not strong enough to perform the duty of presenting the king for coronation. As a result of that, I was chosen to act on his behalf. Ogbuefi explained even as he stood with Okonta who was obviously full of anger.

The presence of Okonta seemed to have instilled calmness on the palace as calmness returned to the place. His supporters quickly got him seated in the King's seat waiting for the crown to be placed on his head. Okechi stood and greeted every one. He paused momentarily and continued as an uneasy calmness settled in the palace.

He greeted again and heaved a sigh of grief. "It is morally despicable and dishonorable that we could not accord due respect to the tradition of the land. I will be strong enough to put the crown on who you have presented. I crave your indulgence to wait until our king emerges for the coronation," Okechi declared and returned to his seat.

Ogbalu sprang from his seat and moved to where the crown was kept. He grabbed the crown from the table. To the amazement of all in the palace, he raised the crown and showed it round to the Kingmakers and mounted the pavilion where Okonta was sitting. He greeted the people and got a heavy ovation in return. After a momentary silence, he greeted again and received the same response. He saluted the third time and got the assurance of the peoples' support before he stepped forward and placed the crown on Okonta's head saying, "No one man is the Itueze. We all made up the body. When one man refuses to carry out a duty assigned him as a member, another member can carry out the duty." He paused and continued.

"Okonta the great warrior, from the great things you have done in our land we are sure that the Kingdom is in safe hands with you as the King. Therefore, we repose the responsibility of overseeing affairs of this kingdom, being the intermediary between members of this kingdom and our ancestors, ensuring the security of the land and people dwelling on it. On behalf of the body of Ituezes, the palace, the clan leaders and the community at large, I hereby bestow the power and authority of the Royal King of Ukpaghari on you. From today, our ancestors, all the people of the land would acknowledge your position as the King of Ukpaghari."

Flanked by Ogbuefi representing the Isieye and Ogbalu representing the Itueze, Okonta majestically moved from his seat to the seat of the exulted crowned King of Ukpaghari kingdom where he had the heads of the various clans that made up the kingdom seated by his sides.

When he got seated with all the paraphernalia of the Royal crown, the palace orator stood and greeted the people of Ukpaghari and began to address the people:

"I greet you all my Lords! Our King has emerged. The great King Okonta-nwa-Otamba has closed the gap that existed in our land for so long. The hole that had lingered in the heart of our land has been healed. According to our tradition, the leader of the Itueze would proclaim the name of the King before all and sundry in the palace. On that note, may we invite the leader of Itueze to announce the name of the King?" The orator retired to his seat after the brief speech.

In compliance with the request, Ogbalu quickly stood up from his seat and prostrated before the new king before turning to speak to the people. "The new king remains His Royal Majesty, King Okonta-nwa-Otamba—the Great Warrior of Ukpaghari. The man that even lions tremble on sighting his presence in the jungle"

There was an eruption of noise in the palace

immediately his name was announced. Many people in the palace applauded the selection of the great warrior as the king while some conservatives frowned at it.

Iwuoha, the palace orator who was standing, remained astonished. He was biting his finger and faced down without uttering a word for some time. When he looked up, he kept probing faces of the elders, clan heads and other members of the palace. He shook his head dispassionately as a sign of disappointment and helplessness. He began, "Ehmmm, the elders have watched helplessly while the goat delivers on its tethers. The land has been desecrated by men of war. It is incredible that we have accepted an abominable act against the tradition of our land"

It was like a sword pierced Ogbuefi's heart as Iwuoha continued with the sarcastic remark. He looked sideways on everybody in the palace. Some members were supporting Iwuoha while other expressed shock and disappointment in the remarks.

Without waiting further, Ogbuefi bellowed: "You are speaking before the lords of the land. Check your tongue not to speak ill of the king"

Iwuoha ignored his warning and continued.

"The land has been desolated and left forlorn. The King has been stripped of royalty. The crown has become a thing of valour and might. We shall ever weep for our land."

Okonta watched helplessly as Iwuoha ridiculed his crown. Ogbuefi warned him again to desist from desecrating the throne. It was at this time that Okonta who had been keeping quiet, decided to urge Iwuoha against his course.

In a more regal tone Okonta informed Iwuoha of the imminent consequence of what he was doing. "More of this assault on the throne would be regrettable to you and your collaborators," Okonta warned. The warning was like a macabre message that suppressed Iwuoha's onslaught. Iwuoha stood stunned with sticky sweat trickling down his back. He knew what Okonta was capable of doing at the slightest provocation.

Okonta seldom gave out warning without a corresponding action. He believed in action than words and one would expect him to act under such provocation. They knew that he would act as he had warned.

Irrespective of his knowledge of the imminent danger, Iwuoha summoned courage to continue with his words. "People of Ukpaghari" Iwuoha continued. "It is not strength of the tongue that protects it from the teeth. I would rather obey the authority and save my head than give my head at the detriment of my family. The mighty men of the land had crowned Okonta-nwa-Otamba as the king of Ukpaghari. The palace from today accepts his power and authority as the king of Ukpaghari."

The pronouncement did not go without the expected pandemonium. Some members of the palace were happy and heralded the king with ovation while others were agitated. After the momentary uproar, Iwuoha invited the seer to foretell the minds of the ancestors over the matter.

In his usual revered arrogance, Okafor the priest shunned the palace commotion as he intimately communed with the ancestors. His eyes were painted with white chalk. His right hand was painted black while the left was white. He carried a raffia bag, a bow and arrow.

The palace became gravely calm as the old man walked into the center of the hall trembling. His two servants were carrying raffia bags and feathers of various birds and cow horn that were stuck on animal skulls. The two lads were not of mundane dispositions. They were half naked, with their eyes painted with white chalk. Walking in their air of sacredness, they settled at the center of the palace with the priest.

Everybody stood up in reverence of the priest as they took the centre stage. The Priest looked sideways at the people and indignantly shook his head. Gazing deeply at Okonta, he began to make an incantation. After a series of incantations, he thundered like a roaring lion, calling on the gods of the land to appear.

"Kamalu agbaramini, the god of gods. Your

children want to hear from you. They have done what they did in ignorance, but you know more than them. Now tell what you have for them"

He looked around, and then to the floor where he selected a position where he sat down, and spread his feet. His servants kept the feathers and the skulls at his left hand side. "Aha!" He exclaimed on seeing what the boys did. He gave the boys a stern look, indicating an error in the placement of those paraphernalia of divination. The Priest muttered some words and removed the skull and feathers, placed them in his front, then rummaged in his raffia bag and brought a small calabash and seven pieces of crystal stones. He put the stones on the calabash and returned to his bag and brought out a small container of liquid which he took a gulp, and then returned the container into the bag.

Everybody concentrated on the Priest as he rolled the crystal stones on the floor and made some incantations before gathering them again. Then threw them again on the floor and studied the setting and shook his head. He uttered some word and into his bag and brought out sculpture, waved it round the stones before gathering them again. He threw them again on the floor and began to count them "mbu, abuo, atoo, ano, ise..."and cleared his throat. "I will say it" he uttered and raised his voice to speak.

"Ehm! Royal people of Ukpaghari, the king

of Ukpaghari, you shall live" This affirmative utterance seemed to gladden Okonta as he beamed a smile "This is exactly what I expected from you," Okonta replied. The Priest ignored him and turned towards the clan rulers and continued.

"Great people of Ukpaghari, the gods have received your message. They will respond on the seven moon festival" he concluded and stood from the floor as his servants began to pack the materials into the raffia bag.

CHAPTER TWELVE

Grief and gaiety were two emotions that swept through the royal homes of Ukpaghari. There was a deep and penetrating air of grief which swallowed the homes of Ukpandu following the enthronement of Okonta as the king of Ukpaghari. The entire compound of the former King Ikpeoha was engulfed in grief. Even those passing by could not avoid pitying the family of the Ikpeoha. Those who could not withhold their tears would shed them for the family. They mourned the rape of tradition in the altar of valour.

Ukpandu's friends came together to console and mourn with him. His only wife, Nneka had also rescinded her movement to the side of his husband. She was sobbing as well as consoling her husband, discouraging him from further quest for the stool. His friends did not agree with his wife concerning the quest for the stool. They posited that the inheritance of a prince cannot be forgone on a flimsy reason of being hijacked by men of valour. "We shall fight on until the tradition of our land would be upheld" Nwosu and Ahamefule insisted. "How can I forget my inheritance, or can I blame my 'chi' who made me the heir to the throne?" Ukpandu lamented. His tone was cracked with cry as he was highly embittered and it showed in his face.

Nneka   frowned   at   her   husband's

determination to fight for the inheritance. She held his hands and consoled him saying, "Nature and the gods have conspired against us. We cannot fight the battle of the gods better than the gods." Ukpandu kept mute and remained tied to the wife.

Ukpandu's posture made mockery of the parlour that was regally furnished by the former king. He seldom used the big parlour except when he had some highly placed visitors. He kept it for the time he would be properly crowned as the king of Ukpaghari.

He avoided the monarch's chair hoping to occupy it after his coronation. Even when it was obvious that he would be enthroned, he decided to maintain the status of the Prince until he was enthroned. Ahamefule and Nwosu were people of the same quality with Ukpandu. They had never gone to any war in the kingdom. They only go where there would be merriment. In their youth days, people of the kingdom use them metaphorically for weaklings. It was believed that even girls could defeat any of them in any wrestling contest.

Though they were agitating for a combat with Okonta over the throne, they would simply catch fever if Okonta noticed them. Nwosu had been discouraging Ukpandu from accepting the crown. He had wished his friend would remain a common man. But Ukpandu's regrets and cries made them to agitate for the crown. After a second thought, Nwosu began to caution Ukpandu against his insistence on regaining the crown.

Amidst all suggestions, tears were still trickling down Ukpandu's cheeks as he continued pondering over the crown. The tears struck anger in Ahamefule who stood and moved as if he would challenge Okonta to a physical combat. 'Aham' as he was fondly called by his friends, was made a little different from Ukpandu. He used to fight in the public although he never won in any of the fights. He exhibited that tendency as he got charged for a fight with whoever was responsible for the calamity that had befallen his friend.

After a moment of anger, Aham remained calm for a while and abruptly exclaimed; "all is not spoilt, we can fight back at the festival of seventh moon."

"You can do what? Please count my husband out of any battle with Okonta" Nneka snapped at him.

Ukpandu cleared the tears that was dripping down his cheeks with the back of his palm and stared on Ahamefule. "I cannot fight the battle of the gods. If our ancestors wish to uphold the institutions they established, so be it"

Ahamefule disliked Ukpandu's answer as he scratched his forehead, stamping his right foot on the floor. "It is incredible that man would watch robbers looting his treasures in the broad day light."Aham cried.

Ukpandu heaved a deep breath of grief. "Chie!" he exclaimed, "Ewu atam igu na isi. My morning has turned to night."

Tears were still rolling down his cheeks as he petitioned, "Ikpeoha my father; I wander if you'll watch the men of valour as they rob me of my inheritance. Gods of our land, could you watch in silence as your land is robbed in your presence? Could it be that my ancestors have no wrath to vent on the murders of our tradition? Woe unto the womb that gave birth to these men that have conspired to rob our land. May the people that desolated our land be swept out of the surface of the land? Those who collaborated to snatch the crown from me shall be snatched out of living.

"Iseee" Ahamefule and Nwosu chorused in agreement with the prayers of Ukpandu.

CHAPTER THIRTEEN

Ukpaghari sailed through tempestuous weather from the inception of Okonta's reign. Various groups that made up the kingdom were at loggerhead with each other. Some of the groups had paid a solidarity visit to the king whereas others vowed never to pay allegiance to his rulership. Even some members of the palace who felt that the enthronement of Okonta as the king was not a good decision withdrew their membership of the palace. However, Okonta was able to force all groups into being loyal to his throne.

The crises lingered till the seventh moon. Seventh moon festival was remarkable in that it was the end of the year. Farmers used to celebrate their harvest after the year's farming season. They would gather at the square to receive the decree of the monarch as well as display their loyalty to the crown.

Festival of seventh moon was a ceremony of re-union. The king would reunite with members of the kingdom whereas the entire community reunites with the ancestors. Daughters would visit their uncles and siblings where they would return with a lot of gift items.

Part of the festivity were rituals that would be made in various shrines to appease the gods and invite them to the festival. Family heads would perform the rituals on behalf of every member of the extended family. Domestic animals such as goats, cocks, sheep and other animals would be slaughtered for the rituals.

Okonta had performed the ritual for his family and the community at large. He had also performed other rituals as the king of the land. These rituals were part of the requirement to qualify the king to appear before the people as the monarch. More so, the priest would be requested to commune with the gods and seek their permission for the king to appear before the people and declare the mind of the ancestors for the year in view.

Ogbuokoiri had been Okonta's seer prior to his ascension to the throne. Okonta retained him as result of his truthful services to Okonta. He had never predicted a thing and it failed to happen. In most cases, he would urge Okonta to do something that would lead to Okonta's glories. He was seeing something different today as Okonta was preparing to appear before the people for the first time.

"Incredible", Okonta cried after getting a negative message from the ancestors. He quickly sent for Ogbuefi and Ogbalu to hear the damning message from the seer. Ogbuokiri was furiously conjuring the gods to appease the ancestors who had declared a war with the kingdom when Ogbuefi and Ogbalu hurriedly walked into the palace.

Ogbuokiri himself was much perturbed about the message from the ancestors. He had made efforts to appease them but to no avail. His face was full of anxiety as his efforts could not appease the ancestors who remain resolute at fighting with the king. Okonta was much infuriated that Ogbuokiri could not get good news from the ancestors. He threatened to deal decisively with Ogbuokiri for conniving with his enemies to sweep him out of the throne.

"Far be it that I will ever turn against the finger that fed me. What would be my benefit if I would lie to my lord and enjoy his favour" Ogbuokiri said.

"The king is not in good mind, so you should not mind his action. Please tell us what the gods said about today" Ogbuefi urged him.

Ogbuokiri shook his head as sorrow and fear clouded his eyes that he could not look up to Okonta. His mind full of pity for Okonta because of the message he got from the gods.

"Tell us" Ogbuefi insisted.

"The gods are angry against my king and the land of Ukpaghari. *Kamalu agbara mini* has vowed to fight against the land today. The gods are angry" Ogbuokiri kept repeating the statement.

Ogbalu and Ogbuefi were shocked by the statement. They were struck with awe because of what the message portended.

"Tufia" Ogbuefi shrugged his shoulder in awe. Ogbalu remained calm for a while and urged Ogbuokiri to advise them on how to appease the gods.

"The king" Ogbuokiri said.

"What did you say" Okonta thundered. "Tell me before I strike you dead" Okonta quickly got up from his seat and rushed into his room and returned with a very sharp machete.

Ogbuokiri remained silent and calm as Okonta who was fuming angrily gazed sternly at him with the machete in his hand. He spoke gently saying, "If the king would kill me to appease the gods, I will willingly offer myself for the sacrifice, but the problem is that such will not solve the problem"

"What exactly shall we do" Ogbuefi asked

Ogbuokiri looked at him apologetically.

"Can I talk to the king in private?" he demanded.

"Far be it that I shall hide anything from Lords of this land. Say whatever you want to say right here and now" Okonta bellowed.

"The gods want you to relinquish the kingdom to Ukpandu for he is the divine king of the land"

"Did you hear him, they have hired him to fight against my throne" Okonta lamented and raised the machete to strike Ogbuokiri.

"Abomination" Ogbuefi exclaimed and held

Okonta by hand to stop him from committing murder.

Okonta's eyes had turned red while his arteries were charged for action. He was ready to sever Ogbuokiri's head from the body before the gods take their disastrous actions. Ogbuokiri was standing motionlessly as Okonta was looking at him like a lion that was targeting an antelope as a prey.

After a long gaze at Ogbuokiri, Okonta called his guards and ordered them to keep him tied in a dungeon until the end of the seventh moon festival. Okonta who was in a fit of anger thundered endlessly like a howling hyena descending.

"War has begun," Okonta declared as he called two other strong looking guards and directed them to run to "Mbaukwu" and bring in those alien soldiers that fight with gun.

"Run, tell them that I Okonta-nwa-Otamba sent you to them. Go at once." He commanded his guards not to return without the soldiers as the people want to revolt against his throne.

CHAPTER FOURTEEN

Mbaukwu was a little distance away from Ukpaghari. People from Ukpaghari and other communities used to converge at the Mbaukwu market with their farm produce for an exchange with iron currency. Here, those alien white men that came from where nobody can tell, used to come once a while to gather the farm produce supplied by many communities and take them to their land.

The white men were said to be great fighters that equip themselves with enormous power that was in an iron metal that sounded like thunder *"kamalu egbelu."* With the power of the iron they could kill many people at once without coming close to the person or engaging the person in a physical combat. They also had men that wore uniform who were trained to handle these weapons. As a result of this power, the white men were dreaded in Mbaukwu and its environs.

Other white men were going around the communities grabbing people and telling them about an unseen God who they believed created the world. They were advising people to abandon their gods and join the unseen God.

And in most cases, they would gather the lazy ones, especially those that could not get valuable harvest from the farms and begin to teach them what nobody else could understand. They would sing songs, clap their hands and dance around like the *'efulefi'* good-for-nothing people.

These white men had visited Okonta through one of their followers from Mbaukwu and promised to support him when he was made the king of Ukpaghari. They came with various gift items and some people who could interpret their language to Okonta. They were escorted by those trained fighters that had the iron that could kill plenty of people at a single eruption.

Okonta had sent his guards to Mbaukwu to fetch those trained warriors to support him in case the people and their gods wish to revolt against his throne.

CHAPTER FIFTEEN

The wooden drum had been beaten to announce the readiness for the festival to begin. Members of the palace had performed the rituals before fetching the *Ikenga* for the king to decree to the people. The *Ikenga* which was the insignia of authority would stand between the people and the ancestor. Holding the ikenga would give the king authority over the living and the dead.

Okonta had not touched the ikenga since he took over the rulership of the kingdom. He had only been ruling over the people through his might. People were wondering if he would set aside the ikenga in this festival of seventh moon. But he would be dethroned if he eventually appeared before the people without the ikenga. It must be used in decreeing to the people else whatever he would utter may not be binding on the people and the gods. Okonta had an inkling of what would happen at the public appearance and he was ready to deal with anybody that would lead a rebellious group whether human or spirit.

Ogbalu and Ogbuefi were waiting in the parlour as Okonta quickly went into the room to get dressed for the ceremony. Inside the room, he saw a creature that was sitting on a wooden chair. The creature was speechless as Okonta breezed into the room.

"Who is there" Okonta retorted. He did not get any answer. Okonta was enraged and dashed to crush the creature. On getting to the creature, the person started sniveling.

"Ah what is the matter?" Okonta asked. "Onunu ugum, what is your problem" he queried. *Onunu ugu* which was the tender part of the vegetable metaphorically used as Tender One. That was one of the pet names Okonta used for his only daughter, Uredi. He was very fond of her that he usually treated her with all amount of sentiment and tenderness. "What on earth would be troubling my beautiful daughter?"

Uredi was the belle of her contemporaries. Very rich in beauty with tick lips, little bow legs that complemented her full hips and full breast, she was considered the most beautiful and alluring damsel in the kingdom. But Uredi was not for the poor, as she was the most pricey Princess at the moment. Okonta's wives used to be jealous of her because Okonta accorded her most respect and regards among all women in the kingdom. They often accuse Okonta of spoiling her by his priceless love to the young lady.

Uredi equally loved her father. She used to whisper to her friends that she would love to marry a young man that would have all the features of her father. She had seen the trouble in her father's face and had devised a means to attract his attention and calm his nerves.

Uredi, Okonta's daughter

When Okonta gave her the desired attention by going to ask what was troubling her, she stopped crying and looked into his father's eyeball. "Papa, it's about my dream last night" she said. Okonta sighed and made to leave her.

"When did you become a dreamer, maybe you were over fed before going to sleep" Okonta whispered.

"Not so father, everything was alright with me until I slept off. I ate moderately and did not have any problem before sleeping off."

"Okay, what was the dream? Just say it quickly because you can see that I am already late to the ceremony" Okonta stated.

"I hate remembering it, but I must let you know about it" Uredi began to narrate her dream. "When I was asleep, I saw a very high mountain that covered the entire land of Ukpaghari in my dream. The mountain caused pandemonium in the land that everybody was seeking for help. The people came out in their multitude to dig and remove the mountain. But it was a herculean task as the people could not dig an inch around the mountain. Then all of a sudden, there was an abrupt flare-up on the mountain that caused it to dissolve into ashes."

Eruption on the mountain

Okonta listened diligently as Uredi narrated her dream, and he burst out laughing. "There is no problem. You were only thinking about the seventh moon festival and dreamt about the land," Okonta responded to the dream.

"This is not my first time of witnessing the festival and I had never dreamt about it before," Uredi insisted.

"Okay, let it be that now that I am the king, I will be able to overcome all the problems of the land," he explained and went ahead to dress up for the ceremony.

Okonta was now dressed in full regalia of the King as he returned to the parlor. Ogbuefi and

Ogbalu who were patiently waiting for the king, quickly stood and bowed in obeisance to the king. As Okonta got seated on the royal chair, he fetched a keg of palm wine that was kept at the center and wanted to pour it in a cup. Ogbuefi quickly rose and took the keg of wine from the king, "How could the king do this when we are here," he said and filled the cup with palm wine and gave it to Ogbalu for libation. Ogbalu held the cup of wine in his hand, conjuring the spirit of their forefathers to intervene in their first outing to the public. He would declare an intention and pour some drops of the wine on the ground and wait for corresponding chorus from the king and Ogbuefi before he would declare another intention.

The time of pouring libation was considered a time being spent with the spirit world. No distraction would be allowed when one was having a time with the spirits. When Ogbalu was pouring the last drop of the wine to the ground, one of the king's guards rushed into the parlor. Okonta ignored him and focused on the libation until it was rounded off. Then he turned to the guard and gave him a rebuking look before querying him about his mission in the palace at the moment.

"My king it is the women," the guard said as he panted.

"What is wrong with the women? Talk,

coward" Okonta thundered." Ogbalu and Ogbuefi were dismayed and dumbfounded.

"The women are chanting war songs and moving all around the villages," the guard reported. Before the king and his men could decipher the message, another guard ran into the parlor.

"Yes what is it again?" Okonta asked.

The second guard explained that the seven age groups were chanting war songs and they were approaching the square where the king was supposed to address the people peacefully.

Okonta turned to Ogbalu and Ogbuefi, probed their face and asked, "Did you hear what I have heard?"

"We are here with you," Ogbalu responded. He stood up from the seat and beat his chest, saying "I, Okonta-nwa-Otamba had never lost any battle in life, even if the whole world would gang up against me, I will surely win the war"

He directed the guards to organize themselves as they were moving to the village square immediately

"Could this be a kind of mutiny?" Ogbalu asked.

"Wait a minute, did I hear the guard saying that women were chanting war songs?" Okonta queried.

"Yes he did," Ogbuefi answered.

"Oh our land is finished. In a land where

women chant war songs, what would their men do? Perhaps, the men would cook their food and take care of the chores, look after the babies as well. No matter what would be the case, I will definitely pluck their feathers today."

"I am hearing some strange sounds. Are those rebels approaching the compound?" Ogbalu asked.

Okonta called the guard that was waiting at the door.

"I am here my lord" he appeared before the king.

"Now quickly run to the gate and bring me a word" he instructed the guard.

The guard quickly ran to the gate and returned with the message that the fighters from Mbaukwu had arrived. He said that they were large in number wielding the magical irons that would kill many people from a distance. Okonta appreciated their prompt arrival and moved to meet with them. They would move together to the village square.

CHAPTER SIXTEEN

The women leader had been silent over the happenings in the kingdom. She was waiting for the festival of the seventh moon for necessary actions to be taken. Before the first cock crow, everywoman in the kingdom had left home, leaving everybody oblivious of their whereabouts. Onyema, the palace spokesman had discussed with Mgbogho the women leader, intimating her how Okonta and his cohorts desecrated the land, arrogated the throne to themselves, and threatening to deal with their men and their gods.

Women seldom lend their voices to matters of the kingdom. The place of the woman was the kitchen and bearing children to the men. Nobody would anticipate any reaction from the women when a sensitive issue about the land arose. In view of this, nobody had any inkling of their reactions to what was amiss in the land.

The King had arrived at the palace under strict guard of the fighters from Mbaukwu. He was meeting with the Isieyes and Ituezes prior to the public appearance and decreeing to the people, when the women marched to the place. Mgbogho the women leader sent a message from the women to Okonta, demanding his immediate relinquishing of the throne to the heir apparent, otherwise every woman in the kingdom would be led out of their homes forever.

They were armed with palm fronds, and other leaf types, still chanting war songs and branding Okonta with derogatory names inimical to his person. Some of the women were shouting that Okonta had polluted the tradition, challenging him to come out and fight the women if he thought he was man enough.

Okonta's guards engaged the women, beating and inflicting wounds on some of them while others ran for their lives. However, the women regrouped at the Community square after the initial beating and were more prepared for a war with the guards and any other force in the land.

They were singing and dancing around the square:

"Is the kingship contestable?"

"No, it is not contestable."

"Can one man be stronger than the entire community?"

"No, one man cannot be stronger than the community."

"Can wealth make the king?"

"No, wealth cannot make the king."

"Can power make the king?"

"No, power cannot make the king."

"Are the kings born to be kings?"

"Yes, kings are born."

The women insisted that kings are born and cannot be enthroned by virtue of their possessions.

While the women were chanting the song, various age groups of the youths and elders were parading around the kingdom, threatening to die for the tradition which Okonta and his cohorts had desecrated. The community was left in confusion.

Iwuoha, Oyia and Okechi had absented themselves from the palace sacrifice prior to the public appearance. Other members of the palace who were loyal to Ukpandu equally absented themselves from the ceremony. Okonta noted the absence of these men with a remark that they were the brains behind the rebellion.

Okonta had directed that the fighters from Mbaukwu should man the strategic positions to avert any possible attack by the rebellious groups. Sango who was their leader was in charge of the pavilion from where Okonta would decree to the people. Other fighters had apprehended leaders of the various groups and kept them in the palace dungeon. The fighters and the palace guards fought gallantly to suppress the revolt. Other fighters from Mbaukwu had arrived to back up the first batch. They all fought to calm the situation

Ogbalu was the first person to speak in order to bring the people back to the authority of Okonta the king. He mounted the rostrum and began to speak:

"Great people of Ukpaghari, I greet you all,"

then, he paused for a second. "When a community stays without war, it would look like the people were not living. The Community had not been without one. We had fought both great and small communities and had been at peace most times. As a result of these ups and down, our land had produced men of integrity. Our Ukpaghari has been the greatest among its contemporaries. If this is true, why should we not be proud of the land?" The speaker looked around the people gathered as if expecting an answer to his rhetorical question.

He continued, "We do not have any reason not be proud of the land which had produced great men in all aspects of life. If we are proud of the land, then we should have no reason to call for a war among ourselves knowing well that such will destroy both the land and its inhabitants. Some of our brothers and sisters who were not well informed about the greatness of the land had instigated our women and youths to challenge the authority of this great kingdom." He looked around again as if to pick the culprits from the audience.

He shook his head and continued, "Well, the king shall decide their fate after this ceremony. Who amongst you is not happy that we have chosen a great man like Okonta to rule a great community like Ukpaghari? I think we had made a good choice for the interest of the community.

Okonta had sacrificed his life to protect this community. He had fought wars to protect every man and woman in this community and we chose him to continue the fight for the betterment of the community in both war and peace time."

Pointing towards the new king, the speaker continued to say, "We chose him in the best interest of the people. All he needs from us is our support and loyalty so that we shall make this community great at all times. Please give him all your support and loyalty as the Okonta-nwa-Otamba, the great king of Ukpaghari comes up now to perform his first assignment as the king of Ukpaghari." This was the end of the speech.

He stopped for emphasis and closed the speech with "Chachacha Ukpaghari kwenu!"

His greeting received a great ovation as the people gave a resounding response. The wooden drum was beaten to announce the ascension of Okonta to the throne of Ukpaghari. Okonta jerked up his mountainous body and marched to the royal stand in the podium. Flanked by Ogbalu and Ogbuefi, Okonta raised the *ikenga* which was the insignia of authority to decree to the people.

Okonta lifts the Ikenga

Immediately he opened his mouth to assume the kingship of the community, he felt like an arrow had just pierced his ribs. He shouted, "Who shot me! Who shot me?" Okonta collapsed on the podium and died with the ikenga falling on top of his body.

"Eh Okonta is dead" the people shouted.

There was pandemonium as everybody started running helter-skelter.

Some of the fighters from Mbaukwu felt some mysterious bullets hitting them as they died instantly. Sango the captain of the fighters was left alone as the people were running chaotically.

Fighters from Mbaukwu

Ogbalu quickly took charge of the situation. He made frantic effort to calm the people so that the gods would be immediately appeased. Ogbalu instructed the guards who were visibly terrified to move immediately and release all the people that were held in the dungeon.

The news of Okonta's tragic demise spread throughout the nooks and crannies of the kingdom as the people were scampering all around the place. Cries and woes took over the entire community as the Iroko fell and a pregnant climbed upon it. The people gathered at the community square to mourn Okonta.

Ukpandu had avoided the community square. Rather he was at home with his friends crying their eyes out over the loss of the crown to the men of valour. He knew that the crown would definitely return to him, but never expected it to come so soon. He was at home when the Okonta's guards scampered into his house and broke the news that his attention was quickly needed at the community square. He enquired from the guards if all was well. It was at that point that they informed him about the mysterious demise of Okonta the great one.

On getting to the square, Ukpandu and his followers wept on the death of Okonta the great warrior. He declared a three days mourning of the great warrior Okonta.

When the news that Ukpandu had gone to take back the throne went to the people, everybody rushed to the square to get the first hand information.

From there the King, Ukpandu decreed that the community would appease the gods and cleanse the land with sacrifices so that the gods will not be angry with the community. Indeed the gods are greater that humans. Kings are not made, kings are born. Ukpandu declared before the crowd that cheered him home at the night.

THE END

Glossary:

Igbo   -   English

Achi of Ukpaghari = The big tree that shields Ukpaghari

Aku nwata na agbaya anyamiri = Child's wealth that gives tears

Chacha Ukpaghari kwenu = Salutation

Chi = God

Ikenga = Insignia of authority

Nkwor day = Market day

Nnekudi = First wife in a polygamous family

Nwa nza = Small bird- sparrow

Okonta-nwa-Otamba = Okonta the son of Otamba

Omere-nwanyi-Asaba = Dealt with Asaba woman

Onunu ugum = Tender Vegetable stem

Otaba = Snuff, tobacco